big & SMALL

Original Korean text by Ki-gyeong Lee
Illustrations by Jong-min Kim
Korean edition © Yeowon Media Co., Ltd

This English edition published by Big & Small in 2015
by arrangement with Yeowon Media Co., Ltd.
English text edited by Joy Cowley
English edition © Big & Small 2015

Distributed in the United States and Canada by
Lerner Publishing Group, Inc.
241 First Avenue North
Minneapolis, MN 55401 U.S. A.
www.lernerbooks.com

ISBN: 978-1-925186-02-4

Printed in Korea

The Wolf and the Seven Kids

A story by the Brothers Grimm
retold by Joy Cowley
Illustrated by Jong-min Kim

Once there was a mother goat
who had seven little kids.
The mother goat loved them very much.

6

Mother goat said to her seven kids,
"I must go to the forest
to get us some food.
Don't open the door while I'm away.
The wolf might come to eat you.
The wolf has a scratchy voice,
and he has black hairy feet.
You will easily know him."

Not long after mother goat left,
there was a knock at the door.
"Open the door, little kids!"
said a loud scratchy voice.
"Mommy has some treats for you."

"You are not our mother,"
the kids said to the wolf.
"Your voice is scratchy.
Our mother's voice is soft."

9

The wolf made his voice soft
and then he came back to the door.
Knock! Knock! "Open the door, kids,"
he said in a soft voice. "Mommy's here!
I have some yummy treats for you."

The kids yelled at the wolf,
"Show your foot at the window!"

When the wolf lifted up his foot,
they cried, "You're not our mother!
Our mother has white feet.
You must be the wolf!"

The wolf ran down the road
to the baker's shop.
He poured white flour
over his feet.

Knock! Knock! Knock!

"Open the door, little kids!"
the wolf said in a soft voice.
"It's your Mommy here!
I have some yummy treats for you all."

"Show us your feet!" cried the kids.

The wolf showed his white feet
and the kids opened the door.

WOLF!!!

One by one,
the wolf swallowed six little kids.
He couldn't find the seventh kid
who was hiding in the grandfather clock.

Mother goat walked in and looked around.
"Oh, no! What has happened to my kids?"

The seventh kid crawled out from the clock
and told her mother what had happened.
Shedding tears, mother goat went out
in search of the wolf.

She didn't have to go far.
The wolf was near the house,
lying on his back and snoring.
Mother goat saw his stomach move.
"My kids are still alive!" she said
and she went back to the house
for a scissors and needle and thread.

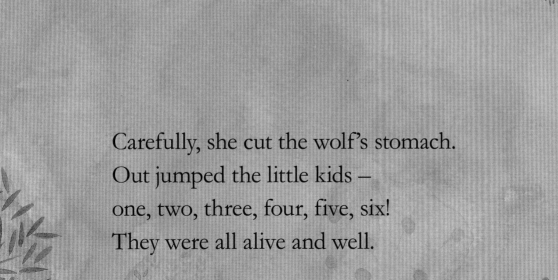

Carefully, she cut the wolf's stomach.
Out jumped the little kids –
one, two, three, four, five, six!
They were all alive and well.

The seven little kids went to the stream
to get some rocks to put in the wolf.
Mother goat sewed his stomach
with the needle and thread.

The wolf woke up.
"Why is my stomach so heavy?"
He walked, clunk, clunk, clunk,
to the stream to get a drink.

He bent over the water
and the weight of the rocks
dragged him off the bank.

SPLASH!

He was gone.

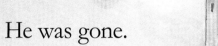

30

Mother goat and the seven kids
began to dance and sing.
"We are safe! We are safe!
The wicked old wolf has gone."